Pick a Pet!

T0337123

Written by Clare Helen Welsh
Illustrated by Sarah Hoyle

Collins

Pick a pet dog.

2

I get a pet.

A pup in mud.

The pugs on mats.

I pick up Meg.

Mum pats the dog.

Mum picks a pen.

I get a mat.

I pick a pot set.

Mum packs ten tins.

Meg naps on the mat.

I got a pet.

/u/

14

After reading

Letters and Sounds: Phase 2

Word count: 50

Focus phonemes: /g/ /o/ /c/ /k/ ck /e/ /u/

Common exception words: the, I

Curriculum links: Understanding the world

Early learning goals: Reading: read and understand simple sentences; use phonic knowledge to decode regular words and read them aloud accurately; read some common irregular words

Developing fluency

- Your child may enjoy hearing you read the book.

- Take turns to read a page. Encourage your child to reread the whole sentence if they have hesitated over the exception words (**the**, **I**) or when blending any sounds.

Phonic practice

- Point to the word **pick** on page 2. Ask your child to sound out and then blend the word. (p/i/ck – **pick**) Check they understand that the capital letter P marks the start of the sentence.

- On pages 6–7, ask them to find the word **Meg**. Next, ask them to find the word **Mum**. Point out the different sounds in the middle of these words (/e/ and /u/).

- On pages 10–11, ask them to find the words that have the /e/ sound. (*set, ten*)

- Look at the "I spy sounds" pages (14–15). Point to the child who is running and say: I spy an /u/ in run. Challenge your child to point to and name different things they can see containing an /u/ sound. Help them to identify /u/, asking them to repeat the word and listen out for the /u/ sound. (e.g. *umbrella, sun, gull, jug, cup, puppy, upside-down*)

Extending vocabulary

- Turn to page 12. Ask your child
  - What other word could you use to describe what the puppy is doing? (e.g. *sleeps, dozes*)